Aaron's Door

Aaron's Door

by Miska Miles

Illustrated by Alan E. Cober

An Atlantic Monthly Press Book
Little, Brown and Company
Boston   Toronto

G816962

Books by Miska Miles

Kickapoo	*Apricot ABC*	*Eddie's Bear*
Dusty and the Fiddlers	*Annie and the Old One*	*Wharf Rat*
See a White Horse	*Mississippi Possum*	*Somebody's Dog*
Pony in the Schoolhouse	*Fox and the Fire*	*Otter in the Cove*
Teacher's Pet	*Rabbit Garden*	*Gertrude's Pocket*
The Pieces of Home	*Nobody's Cat*	*Tree House Town*
Uncle Fonzo's Ford	*Hoagie's Rifle-Gun*	*Swim, Little Duck*
	Chicken Forgets	*Aaron's Door*

TEXT COPYRIGHT © 1977 BY MISKA MILES
ILLUSTRATIONS COPYRIGHT © 1977 BY ALAN E. COBER
ALL RIGHTS RESERVED. NO PART OF THIS BOOK MAY BE REPRODUCED IN ANY FORM OR BY ANY ELECTRONIC
OR MECHANICAL MEANS INCLUDING INFORMATION STORAGE AND RETRIEVAL SYSTEMS WITHOUT PERMISSION
IN WRITING FROM THE PUBLISHER, EXCEPT BY A REVIEWER WHO MAY QUOTE BRIEF PASSAGES IN A REVIEW.

FIRST EDITION

T 04/77

Library of Congress Cataloging in Publication Data

Miles, Miska.
  Aaron's door.

  "An Atlantic Monthly Press book."
  SUMMARY: Unable to adjust to the idea of being
adopted and having a new mother and father, Aaron locks
his door against the world.
  [1. Adoption–Fiction] I. Cober, Alan E. II. Title.
PZ7.M5944Aar   [Fic]   76-41159
ISBN 0-316-57017-6

ATLANTIC–LITTLE, BROWN BOOKS
ARE PUBLISHED BY
LITTLE, BROWN AND COMPANY
IN ASSOCIATION WITH
THE ATLANTIC MONTHLY PRESS

Published simultaneously in Canada
by Little, Brown & Company (Canada) Limited

PRINTED IN THE UNITED STATES OF AMERICA

To Thomas Emory Little

Deep underground in his burrow, snug-lined with dried leaves, a scruffy groundhog curled up tightly, his tail over his head. He slept, waiting for the coming of spring.

Overhead, on the bare twisted boughs of an old apple tree, small, tough buds were swelling with the promise of spring-time.

Nearby, inside a small house, a boy lay on his bunk with his blanket pulled over his head, waiting, waiting — listening for the sound of the knob turning in his door. A door he wouldn't open. A door locked. Locked against everyone.

His stomach muscles twisted into a hard knot.

This was a new home.

Aaron dug his head into his pillow. He remembered the other homes he and his sister Deborah had known.

There was the real one with their own mother and father. The father went away one day and never came back. The mother had rough brown hands and long, soft hair. She left them in the Children's Home. And now, this new home.

When the woman took them around the house — him and Deborah — the woman had said, "This will be your home always."

Aaron knew better. Nothing was always. Nothing would be always for him.

He heard footsteps in the hall.

The knob turned in the door.

"Aaron," the woman called to him. "Aaron, did you lock the door?"

Aaron didn't answer.

The knob turned again — impatiently. "Aaron. Please open the door. Come on down to dinner. Everything's on the table."

Aaron turned his face from the pillow and pushed his blanket away. The knot in his stomach grew tighter.

"Can you hear me, Aaron?"

And then his sister called. "Aaron? Aaron?"

"WHAT." Aaron's voice sounded loud and strange in his ears.

"Come on out, Aaron," Deborah said. "We're having chicken. You like chicken."

"GO AWAY," Aaron said.

The steps went down the hall.

He twisted over, face down, and sobbed, muffling the sound in his pillow.

And then he lay still, without feeling . . .

But soon, feeling washed through him. Anger at Deborah. He hated her. Always putting her arms around the woman's waist. Hugging the man. Calling the man Dad, and the woman Mom. He had nothing. No mother. No father. He hated everyone.

He remembered when the man and woman took them out into the woods. It was fun until they told him that he and Deborah were to be adopted. He had liked the car ride and the food the man cooked over a fire that crackled and snapped . . .

At the thought of food, his stomach turned again.

He hugged himself to quiet its hurting.

There was a loud rap on the door.

The man's voice.

"Aaron, I'm putting your dinner outside here for you. Eat it while it's hot. You'll like it."

Then, silence, and footsteps moved away and down the stairs.

I will never open that door. I will never open that door and no one can make me.

When he heard the clatter of dishes in the kitchen, he crept close to the door and sniffed. He couldn't smell chicken. He listened. There was no sound but the clatter of dishes.

The key was cold in his fingers.

No. If he went outside someone might be waiting. They'd take the key. He didn't want their food.

He flopped down on his bunk again and waited.

After a while there were voices outside again.

"He hasn't eaten a thing," the woman said.

"Let's not hurry him," the man said.

"But Dad — " Deborah was talking. "He'll get hungry."

"Don't worry," the man said. "He'll come out when he's really hungry."

Aaron hated the man's voice.

I hate the way he talks, Aaron thought. I hate the way he looks. Prickly looking, stupid beard. He likes his beard. He keeps brushing it with his fingers. He likes that beard better than anything in the world.

Wobbling a bit, Aaron got out of his bunk and crossed over and leaned his forehead against the cool glass of the windowpane. Moonlight shone silver on the old apple tree.

And underneath, a rabbit nibbled on a bit of weed.

Deep in the ground under the apple tree, the groundhog curled up tightly. Waiting. Waiting.

Everything was still. Strangely still.

Perhaps everyone had gone to bed.

Stealthily, slowly, Aaron turned the key in the lock and looked outside. The food was gone.

Across the hall, the door to the bathroom was closed. Someone was inside. He shut his door and turned the key in the lock.

Safe.

Safe from everything.

Safe from the world.

Aaron thought about the day the man and the woman came to the Children's Home to get them. To bring them here.

The man with the beard had put his hand on Aaron's shoulder. Aaron jerked away and stood as tall as he could stand, with his back hard against the wall.

The man was surprised. He didn't like it. And Aaron was glad.

He remembered how the man had tossed the suitcases in the back of the car and climbed in the front seat without saying anything. They drove a long way, and the woman talked all the time.

"You'll both be going to a nice school. And there's a boy in the house next to ours, Aaron — he's about your age. And you'll each have a room of your own. We've been waiting for you for such a long, long time — "

Aaron had whispered to Deborah. "They want YOU. Remember at the Home? Everybody wanted little kids or maybe a girl. Nobody wanted me."

"They LIKE you, Aaron," Deborah whispered. "And you'll like them back."

"No I won't," Aaron said.

Now he listened to the sounds of this new home — a rattle and a squeak, a soft thud and a scratch. He shivered in his bunk. He missed the sounds of cars and trucks — a little kid yelling in his sleep — someone hurrying to help. Doors opening. Doors closing. Deborah always glad to see him.

Yesterday in this new house, he and Deborah had a fight. He hit Deborah and she fell down and he saw the tears in her eyes.

Afterward, the man talked to him. When Aaron didn't say he was sorry, the man hit the arm of his chair with a fist. Aaron knew what that meant. The man was angry. He really wanted to hit Aaron and he hit the chair instead. The man hated him. And Aaron didn't care. He was glad. He didn't care about anything.

He closed his eyes and he slept.

Morning came. A streak of sunlight crossed the rug. The room felt empty.

When the woman first showed this room to him, she said, "Bunk beds are good for a boy to have. If you have a friend who comes to sleep overnight, you've got a special place for him."

"I don't have friends," Aaron said.

"You will have," the woman promised.

How did she know? I've never had a friend, Aaron thought. I don't even have Deborah. She's on THEIR side.

He looked around the room. The room the woman said was his alone.

There was a chest of drawers with shorts and T-shirts. Jeans. And hanging in a small closet was a jacket. Like the man's. He'd never take that off the hanger. Never ever.

Across the room was a table with shelves above it. Propped up beside the table was a baseball bat. A mitt and a ball lay on the floor beside it. They would stay there.

In the middle of the table was a ship model, red, with many little white sails.

"Dad put that together for you," the woman had said. "And there's another one in that package just like it, and the two of you can fix that one, together."

Not me, Aaron thought. Deborah can. I won't. They can't fool me by giving me things.

After a while he heard noises in the kitchen.

Deborah was laughing.

Aaron clenched his jaw.

He threw himself across the bunk and thumped the mattress with his fists.

Outside his door, the woman spoke.

"Aaron," she said, "I'm leaving breakfast here for you. Cereal and milk. Orange juice. Eat it when you're ready."

Aaron didn't answer.

Her steps tapped along the hall toward the kitchen. The man said goodbye and a door slammed.

That man was going off to work. He didn't care about anyone but himself.

Aaron lay on the bunk — unmoving.

Again, there was a rap.

"Aaron," the woman said, "I'm taking Debbie to school. Eat your breakfast while I'm gone. Please?"

Aaron held his breath.

"Aaron, do you hear me?"

"I hear you," Aaron said. His voice shook.

He heard the kitchen door open. He heard the car start. They were gone.

He thought about opening the door and eating the cereal and drinking the milk. He unlocked the door.

The food.

He looked at it. He thought he was going to be sick. He hurried across the hall to the bathroom. His throat was filled with an ugly yellow taste.

When he returned to his room, he did not want to look at the food.

Trembling, he closed the door and turned the key in the lock.

He couldn't eat their food. He knew he couldn't swallow it. He couldn't sit at the table and eat it as Deborah did. He couldn't hug the man, as Deborah did.

He threw himself across his bunk and he hugged his pillow tightly. He cried, softly . . .

The day was long.

The woman did not come to his door again.

Aaron lay shaking on his bunk, curled up tightly, waiting.

He heard the car leave the yard. That would be the woman going to school to get Deborah.

Aaron's face crumpled but he could not cry. The muscles in his forehead hurt. The bones in his face ached. He clenched his fists until the nails bit into the palms of his hands.

He slid out of bed and crossed the room and picked up the baseball mitt and slid his hand into it.

He lifted his hand high and let it smash down upon the small ship.

Little pieces of plastic flipped over the table and down to the floor.

Aaron dropped the mitt and found that his knees would not hold him. Numb, he slid down on the floor and looked at the shattered pieces.

He touched the broken bits of the little ship. His heart seemed to stop beating.

Then there were noises downstairs.

Deborah and the woman were home.

There was low talk — and Deborah called, "DAD'S COM-ING."

The man entered the house noisily. There were a few quiet words before the man came along the hall. Heavy steps. Threatening steps.

"AARON. OPEN THE DOOR. NOW."

Aaron crouched on the floor.

"ONE MORE CHANCE, AARON. OPEN THIS DOOR."

Then the shattering of wood.

A shoulder came through the broken panel.

A fist followed and a big hand unclenched and turned the key. The door opened.

Aaron couldn't move. Chill spread through his body to his toes, and he huddled on the floor, shivering. He shut his eyes — tight — he felt himself being swooped into the air, his world was ending.

He was caught close against the man's shoulder.

The man's beard scraped his cheek.

Arms held him tightly. Aaron fought, but the arms held.

"Aaron. Aaron." The man spoke softly, softly.

Aaron felt the rock of the man's stride as he was carried along the hall.

Aaron stiffened, pushing hard against the man, and the man stopped.

Afraid, Aaron opened his eyes. The arms released him and Aaron's feet touched the floor. The man walked on.

Slowly, Aaron followed the big feet.

In the kitchen the table was set.

There were the places set for the woman and the man and for Deborah. And there was a place for him.

"Maybe they want me," Aaron thought. "Maybe they still want me."

Beyond the fence, the groundhog came out of his burrow and sniffed the air, warm with the springtime.

He scurried a few steps from his doorway and nibbled new clover.

On the crooked branches of the old apple tree, one little blossom burst its husk. Spring had come.